SOARING SOREN
WHEN FRENCH BULLDOGS FLY

PREFACE

Sometimes people say a thing will happen "when pigs fly." Since pigs almost never fly, they say this to mean that something is unlikely to ever happen—like, "Teddy will eat broccoli when pigs fly." But sometimes, when you truly believe and try as hard as you can, pigs (or in this case, a French Bulldog) really can fly and anything is possible. Such is the unlikely story of how Soren became an agility dog.

Dedication

For Soren, with my deepest love, gratitude and admiration. May your spirit, heart and determination continue to inspire. For three incredible women, without whom there would be no story to tell: Tove supplied the wings, Suzanne added the wind beneath them so we could soar, and Barb taught us how to fly. For Scott, whose love of reading as a child inspired me to write a children's book.

Second Edition, 2018

Book designed by Morgan Spicer

Hardcover ISBN: 978-1-7325410-8-5

Paperback ISBN: 978-1-7325410-9-2

Library of Congress Control Number: 2018955539

SOARING SOREN

WHEN FRENCH BULLDOGS FLY

Deborah Stevenson

Illustrated By Morgan Spicer

Hi. I'm Soren the French Bulldog. I was born in a country called Denmark. When I was a puppy, people said I was quite handsome and that I was going to fly to the United States to become a show dog.

The long, noisy plane ride was a little scary.

When I arrived at the airport, I was relieved to hear a kind voice.

"I've been waiting for you, Soren," said a woman with wild, curly hair. "My name is Deb."

Deb hugged me and said, "You must be hungry. I brought you some French fries."

I knew right then I was going to like my new home.

Once I settled into my new house, we went to work on my show training on the big patio next to the lake.

"To be a show dog, you have to look and act like a dog of your breed should," Deb told me. "You need to trot on a leash, stand tall and let a judge look at your teeth."

I tried hard to be the perfect French Bulldog.

But something happened. I grew, and grew some more.

One day Deb said, "I'm afraid you will not be a show dog after all, Soren. You are growing bigger than a show French Bulldog is allowed to be."

I was sad. I did not want to disappoint Deb. I wished and wished to stop growing, but I could do nothing to stop it.

One morning Deb was sitting on the grass, watching as I ran around the yard jumping over bushes and logs.

She said, "Soren, you can run fast and jump high. I bet you would make a great agility dog!"

I tipped my head—I wasn't sure what that meant.

"The word 'agility' means being quick and graceful," Deb explained. "Agility is also a sport. You run through an obstacle course as fast as you can. French Bulldogs aren't built for speed and grace, so many people think they can't do agility."

Agility! If I couldn't be a show dog, maybe I could be an agility dog!

I wanted to show Deb I could be a great agility dog, so I jumped on and off a big rock.

When Deb threw my favorite tennis ball, I ran as fast as I could, grabbed it, and brought it back.

As I dropped the ball in her lap, I started to feel funny. My tummy began to flip-flop.

Deb's eyes got w i d e. She blurted out, "Uh oh, Soren, *noooo!*"

But before I could stop it... *blaargh!* I threw up—right on Deb!

I thought surely that would be the end of agility. But when I looked up, Deb was laughing.

"It's okay, buddy," she said. "If any French Bulldog can do agility, I think it might be you, Soren."

D eb took me to a place called an agility field. She explained the obstacles to me and I got to try them.

I ran up and over the A-Frame. Deb said my feet had to touch the yellow part.

Jumps seemed pretty simple; I *soared* over the plastic jump bars without knocking them down.

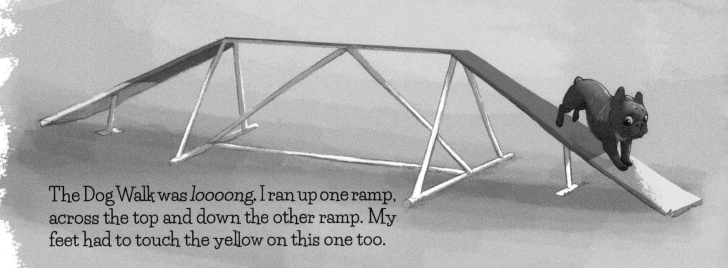

The Dog Walk was *loooong*. I ran up one ramp, across the top and down the other ramp. My feet had to touch the yellow on this one too.

Weave Poles were weird: twelve poles sticking out of the ground. I had to go in the first opening and weave between each pole to the very end.

The Teeter was just like the one at the playground. I ran up one side, made it tip, and ran down the other side, making sure to touch the yellow. *Wheeee!*

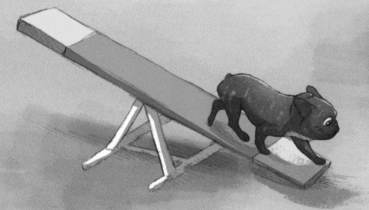

The Tunnel was my favorite. I ran in one end, disappeared, and ran out the other end.

Agility was so much fun!

When I got tired, I stopped and looked up at Deb.

"Okay, Soren," Deb said.
"I guess you will be an agility dog!"

We practiced and practiced agility and learned to work as a team. Deb's job was to learn the course and show me where to go. My job was to go where she sent me and do the obstacles correctly.

Weave poles were the most difficult for me. When I got them right, I got cheese as a treat. Cheese was my favorite!

"Once we are good enough at agility," Deb told me, "we'll go to a sporting competition called an agility trial."

After months of training, it was time for our first trial. Deb brought me to an indoor soccer field, where a course was set up.

There were other agility teams everywhere and the dogs were all so different from me.

They looked faster and more athletic.

"You can do this, Soren!" Deb reassured. "This is just like we practiced."

When it was our turn, we walked out to the first obstacle.

"Sit!" Deb said.

I waited until she said "Go!" and we took off running.

Oops! I was so excited that I jumped off the A-Frame from way up high and did not touch the yellow part. People in the crowd gasped, then cheered when they saw I did not get hurt. I did the rest perfectly —and pretty fast too!

Afterward, a friend told Deb, "Soren did a great job!"

"Maybe someday he'll get an agility championship," Deb replied.

They laughed at that idea, because no French Bulldog had come close to being an agility champion, *ever*. But as I got better at agility, we started thinking maybe I really could be a champion.

"To become a champion, you have to run lots of different courses," Deb explained. "You need to be fast and you can't make any mistakes."

Fast *and* no mistakes? That would be tricky, but I was sure I could do it!

Most people we met at trials were nice. They smiled and said hello to me when I walked by, and cheered me on when I ran the course. But some thought French Bulldogs couldn't do agility.

"SOREN'S NOT FAST ENOUGH TO GET A CHAMPIONSHIP," ONE WOMAN SAID, AND ROLLED HER EYES.

"THEY'RE JUST NOT BUILT FOR AGILITY," I OVERHEARD ANOTHER WOMAN SAY.

"THEIR HEADS ARE TOO BIG, THEIR LEGS ARE TOO SHORT, AND THEIR BODIES ARE TOO HEAVY."

It was true my head was big, and my legs weren't the longest, and I was heavier than other dogs my size, but I could and I *would* do agility!

Deb hugged me close and said, "Don't worry, Soren. We'll show them you *can* do agility."

The more we ran agility, the better and faster I got. On Deb's birthday, we were getting into the car to go to our agility trial.

Deb said, "You know, Soren, if you run fast enough today, you could get your championship!"

More than anything I wanted to give Deb that championship as her birthday gift.

When it was our turn, Deb told me to "sit" in front of the first obstacle. But I was too excited. She understood.

She smiled at me and said "Go!" The rest was magical.

Deb said I needed to be fast to earn my championship,
so I ran as fast as my short legs would carry me. I was
extra careful to touch the yellow on the A-Frame.

Those tricky weave poles were next
and they always worried me.

I pictured myself getting in at just the right spot, and I did! I pushed through them as fast as I could, weaving between every pole, all the way to the end. Just two more jumps to go!

I soared over the last jump bar just in the nick of time!

We did it! People started to cheer.

Deb kissed my cheek. "I knew you could do it buddy!" she said.

The agility judge patted my head. Someone handed Deb a huge ribbon as a prize. Someone else gave her the bar from my final jump. They let us keep the bar as a memento. While everyone clapped, we got to run around the course and do the obstacles again.

Deb gave me a gift:

a pretty new collar with flying pigs on it.
They looked a little like me!

Our friends had a big party for us and tied colorful balloons onto my new collar. We all wore party hats shaped like cheese—my favorite treat. Everyone signed our jump bar and wrote notes on it, telling us what a great team we were. There was a cake, too. I love cake even more than cheese!

Deb said, "This is the best birthday ever, Soren. Now and forever you will be the first French Bulldog to earn an agility championship!"

I could tell Deb was proud of me and I was so happy. I loved agility, but I loved Deb even more.

Sometimes I wonder what life would have been like if I had been a show dog. But then I never would have been an agility dog. I would not trade my amazing agility adventure with Deb for the world.

If you work hard and believe in yourself and your dreams, you can do just about anything. And if you have someone you love who believes in you too, that's better still.

MEET THE REAL SOREN

This book is based on the true story of Soren. He overcame the challenges of his breed to become the first French Bulldog ever to earn a Master Agility Championship (MACH)! Soren actually earned more than ONE HUNDRED performance titles. Despite being a little bulldog, he was quite an athlete. He was ranked among the top agility dogs in the country.

Soren was a loving, devoted, comical character with a joy for life. He won friends everywhere he went with his easy smile, his kind, gentle nature and—most of all—his "can do" attitude.

Soren's story reminds us that we don't have to be limited by stereo-types—the ideas other people might have about what we can and cannot do. He proved that when we work hard and try with all our hearts, we can accomplish things we never dreamed possible.

You can honor Soren by never giving up on your own dreams and by supporting the goals of others. We'll honor him too by donating a portion of the proceeds from this book to French Bulldog rescue. For more information on this, or to see more of the real Soren in action, please visit **www.FrogPrinceBooks.net.**

Acknowledgments

To the highly-talented and creative Morgan: Thank you more than I can say for bringing the magic of Soren's story to life so beautifully on these pages. Thank you to Krista Hill, Richard Slotkin, and Rory Maruschak, for their invaluable input and advice. With thanks to the "other" Deb and our wonderful agility friends—you are such a cherished part of my journey with Soren.

Author Deborah Stevenson and illustrator Morgan Spicer have won numerous awards for their children's books, including Best Children's Non-Fiction Book, Next Generation Indie Book Awards for *Soaring Soren: When French Bulldogs Fly*, and Feathered Quill's Best Children's Animal Book for *Oy, Elephants!* They share a passion for animals that is the heart and soul of their collaboration, and a strong desire to share that passion with children.

Stevenson's books convey positive messages about believing in your abilities—to achieve your goals, to make positive differences in the world, and to be kind to yourself and to others. A former technical writer, literature major and mother, children's books have proven to be a perfect outlet for Deborah's interests. She lives in New Jersey with a few too many dogs, but wouldn't trade any of them. She enjoys training for and competing in the sport of dog agility.

Photo © M. Nicole Fischer Photography

Morgan Spicer believes kindness can make a world of difference in anyone's life, be it a young reader, a parent or a four-legged friend. Vegan and dog mom, Spicer will one day open the doors to a creative and cruelty-free oasis: a place where humans and animals, young and old, can come together every day, to celebrate the beauty of nature and embrace the importance of kindness and compassion. Spicer has illustrated over twenty children's books. She lives in the woods by the beach with her four rescue dogs and her husband.

Photo courtesy of Morgan Spicer

Check out these other books by the award winning team!

Deborah Stevenson

The Last Rhino

Illustrated by Morgan Spicer

From the award-winning author of *Soaring Soren...*

OY, ELEphants!

written by
DEBORAH STEVENSON

illustrated by
MORGAN SPICER

Now available on Amazon as well as FrogPrinceBooks.net

CPSIA information can be obtained
at www.ICGtesting.com
Printed in the USA
BVHW022035161118
533333BV00004B/63/P